The
Kingdom

The
Palace

Burth

Mermaid's
Cove

Crestwood

gdom

Wrenly

=== 20 ===

The Crimson Spy

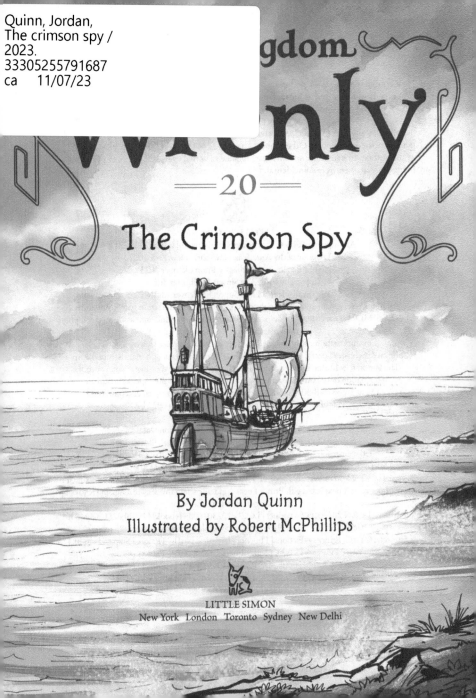

By Jordan Quinn

Illustrated by Robert McPhillips

LITTLE SIMON

New York   London   Toronto   Sydney   New Delhi

LITTLE SIMON

An imprint of Simon & Schuster Children's Publishing Division
1230 Avenue of the Americas, New York, New York 10020
First Little Simon paperback edition October 2023
Copyright © 2023 by Simon & Schuster, Inc.
Also available in a Little Simon hardcover edition.
All rights reserved, including the right of reproduction in whole or in part in any form.
LITTLE SIMON is a registered trademark of Simon & Schuster, Inc., and associated colophon is a trademark of Simon & Schuster, Inc.
For information about special discounts for bulk purchases, please contact
Simon & Schuster Special Sales at 1-866-506-1949 or business@simonandschuster.com.
The Simon & Schuster Speakers Bureau can bring authors to your live event. For more information or to book an event contact the Simon & Schuster Speakers Bureau at 1-866-248-3049 or visit our website at www.simonspeakers.com.
Manufactured in the United States of America 0923 LAK
2 4 6 8 10 9 7 5 3 1
Library of Congress Cataloging-in-Publication Data
Names: Quinn, Jordan, author. | McPhillips, Robert, illustrator.
Title: Crimson spy / by Jordan Quinn ; illustrated by Robert McPhillips.
Description: First Little Simon paperback edition. | New York : Little Simon, 2023.
Series: The Kingdom of Wrenly ; book 20 | Audience: Ages 5–9. | Summary: While caring for a rare phoenix, an unexpected gift, Prince Lucas and Lady Clara investigate a missing royal ship that brings rumors of pirates.
Identifiers: LCCN 2023016084 (print) | LCCN 2023016085 (ebook) | ISBN 9781665948401 (paperback) | ISBN 9781665948418 (hardcover) | ISBN 9781665948425 (ebook)
Subjects: CYAC: Princes—Fiction. | Phoenix (Mythical bird)—Fiction. | Ships—Fiction. | Pirates—Fiction. | Kings, queens, rulers, etc.—Fiction.
Classification: LCC PZ7.Q31945 Cr 2023 (print) | LCC PZ7.Q31945 (ebook) | DDC [Fic]—dc23
LC record available at https://lccn.loc.gov/2023016084

CONTENTS

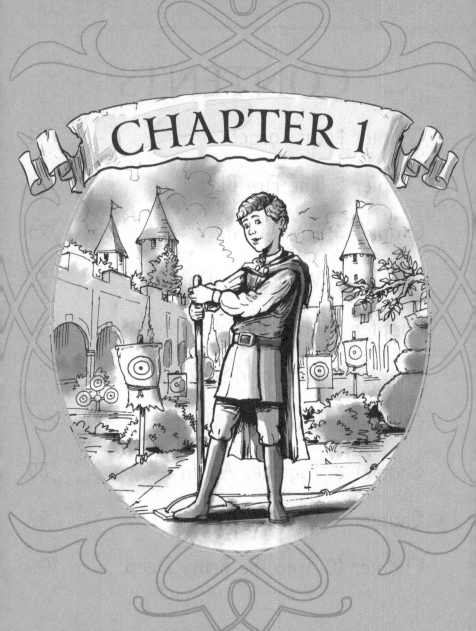

CHAPTER 1

On Target

"Bet you can't hit *these* targets!" Prince Lucas shouted gleefully.

It was the first time his best friend, Clara, was trying out the newest archery course.

The prince pulled on a wooden level, and hidden archery boards popped in and out of sight in the courtyard.

The course had been a challenge for Lucas to build. He hoped it would be a challenge for the archer too.

Clara chose three arrows and raised her bow.

"Three . . . two . . . one . . . FIRE!" the prince shouted.

Clara aimed at a few spinning targets hanging from a tree branch.

Then she released all three arrows at the same time. They whistled through the air before piercing each bull's-eye.

Thwack! Thwack! Thwack!

Lucas hooted and clapped. The palace guards also gave an impressed cheer.

"A perfect shot for *each one!*" Lucas exclaimed. "Incredible!"

Clara twirled her bow with ease. She was becoming one of the best archers in Wrenly.

"This new bow isn't half bad," she said.

Lucas held up his shabby, not-so-new bow. "Beats this scuffed-up one. You'd think I'd have something fancier!"

Clara laughed. "Let's see what that rickety old thing can do."

The kids were resetting the targets when a knight rushed into the courtyard.

He bowed before them and said, "The king requires your presence in the throne room at once."

Lucas and Clara shared a look before following the knight inside the castle. When they reached the throne room, guards pushed open the heavy wooden doors.

King Caleb and Queen Tasha sat upon their golden thrones. Their crowns glittered in the afternoon sunlight. Lucas bowed and Clara curtsied before them.

"What's going on, Father?" Prince Lucas asked.

The king leaned forward with a glint in his eyes. "We've received a most unusual gift from a Nameless Messenger."

"A gift," Queen Tasha added, "which requires you both be here to open it."

Unusual gifts weren't new in the castle. From magical flowers to orbs bursting with prophecies from the Hobsgrove wizards, the royal family had seen it all.

What *was* strange, however, was that Lucas and Clara needed to be there to receive it.

The king snapped his fingers. "Come forth, Nameless Messenger, and deliver our gift."

CHAPTER 2

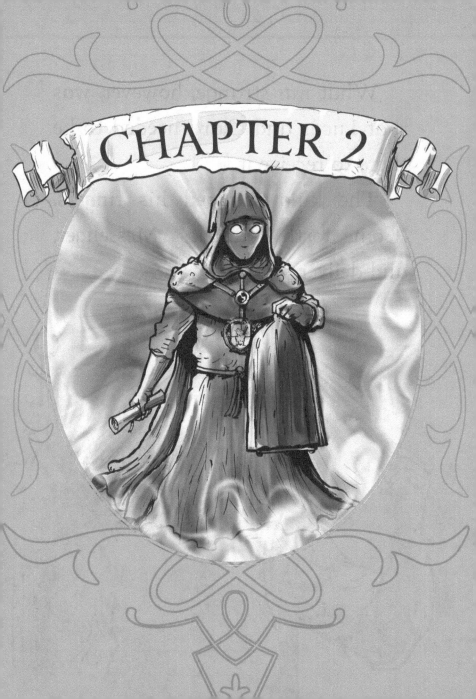

The Fire Bird

A dark, shadowy figure swirled from the corner of the room and approached the thrones.

Whoa . . . so that's what a Nameless Messenger looks like, Lucas thought in awe.

Not much was known about Nameless Messengers, except for three things.

First, they often delivered strange packages.

Second, they were beings of few words and bowed to no one.

And lastly, it was unknown whether a visit from one brought a gift . . . or a curse.

This Nameless Messenger wore a dark uniform and a faceless mask. Moving soundlessly in a billow of smoke, he carried a large package covered in black cloth. Something rustled from within.

The Nameless Messenger handed King Caleb a scroll, stepped back, and removed the black cloth from the gift. A grand, gilded cage was revealed, holding a very magical being.

Clara gasped. "It's a phoenix!"

A halo of fire crowned the beautiful bird. Its scarlet and gold feathers glimmered in the sunlight.

"Wow, these are very rare," said Lucas. "I never expected to see

one . . . much less be given one!"

King Caleb waved his hand. "Thank you, Nameless Messenger. That will be all."

The Nameless Messenger disappeared in a spiral of smoke.

Lucas and Clara kneeled before the cage. They both wanted to touch the beautiful bird, but phoenixes were birds of fire.

"Who would send us such a gift?" Lucas asked. "Does it say?"

King Caleb untied the scroll and quickly read through it. "There is no mention of a sender, but there is a message."

Lucas hopped to his feet. "What does it say?"

"It states that you and Clara must take care of the phoenix," said King Caleb.

Clara's eyes grew wide. "But we don't know how to take care of a magical creature."

"Except for Ruskin, but that's different," Lucas pointed out. "We got Ruskin when he was still an egg."

"This is no different," Queen Tasha kindly said.

"May I see the scroll, My King?" Clara asked. The king handed it over. Clara read it aloud:

"By growing light and sorrows,

The prince and lady must guard

The embers of red tomorrows,

And hopes and dreams left charred."

Lucas frowned. "What does that mean?"

King Caleb stroked his chin.

"I do not know," the king admitted. "But I'm sure it will become clear in time. For now, make the phoenix feel at home."

Lucas peered into the cage. The shimmering phoenix flapped his red-and-gold wings.

"What's your name?" Lucas asked.

The bird opened his beak and let out a sizzling hiss.

Lucas tried to imitate the sound. "Zishess?"

The phoenix chirped at the sound of his name.

Lucas and Clara smiled.

"Welcome to the kingdom of Wrenly, Zishess!" the prince said. "Your new home."

CHAPTER 3

THE ROYAL LIBRARY

Fire Alarm!

If there was one place to learn about phoenixes, it was the royal library. That's where Lucas and Clara headed as soon as possible.

The royal library was like a huge treasure chest, and the books in it were precious gems.

In the rare book room, Lucas placed Zishess's cage beside the

fireplace to keep the phoenix warm. Magical vines kept the books locked in place on the shelves. With permission from the librarian, the vines uncurled so the kids could look at the books.

Lucas and Clara gathered three thick volumes titled *Creatures of the Unknown*, *Fire-Breathers*, and *Mystical Birds*. Sitting in a cozy corner near Zishess, they pored over the pages.

"This says phoenixes are wise and fiercely loyal creatures," Clara said. "They love to soar near the sun and spend hours sunbathing."

Lucas flipped through the pages of *Mystical Birds*. "This says phoenixes only eat red fruits and vegetables, like strawberries, beets, and watermelon. Red foods add color to their feathers." Zishess chirped in approval.

Clara gazed at the beautiful phoenix. Feeling brave, she reached her hand into the cage and gently petted Zishess's head. The feathers felt warm but not hot. The phoenix leaned into Clara's hand.

"I think he likes me!" she said.

Lucas laughed and, at the same time, something nearby growled. The kids looked up to see Ruskin, the prince's red dragon. He approached them slowly, low to the ground.

"Don't worry, Ruskin," Lucas said. "Zishess is our new friend."

Ruskin sniffed the cage and

growled again. The phoenix pecked
the bars, and a flame swirled from
his crest. Ruskin reared back and
roared. The vines on the rare books
clamped tightly around the spines.

Lucas leaped to his feet. "Ruskin,
stop!"

The red dragon held in his fire,

but smoke curled from his nostrils.

Clara blocked Zishess's cage. "Whoa, what was *that* all about?"

Normally, Ruskin was a kind and gentle dragon.

The librarian rushed over. "Your Highness! The royal library is *no place* for fire-breathing creatures!

Our rare books could be burned to ashes with one fiery sneeze!"

Lucas guided Ruskin away from the shelves. "I'm sorry. I'll take him back to my room. Clara, could you please take Zishess outside for some fresh air?"

Clara picked up the birdcage and looked at the phoenix. Their eyes locked, and a strange feeling swept over Clara. Suddenly, she didn't want to do as Lucas asked.

"Zishess is an enchanted creature," Clara said with a sudden sneer. "He doesn't belong with pigeons, owls, and ravens. He's better off in the throne room."

Lucas looked surprised at her sudden shift but shrugged. "I suppose it wouldn't hurt for my parents to keep an eye on him."

The phoenix cooed with approval. Ruskin narrowed his eyes suspiciously.

And when the kids left the library, the librarian let out a long sigh of relief.

CHAPTER 4

What's Up, Dock?

Tap! Tap! Tap! Clara sat up in bed and rubbed her eyes.

That's funny, she thought. *I don't remember coming home last night. Wasn't I just dropping off Zishess in the throne room?*

Tap! Tap! Tap!

Clara hopped out of bed to open her door.

It was Lucas, and he looked upset.

"*There* you are!" he said. "I've been sending messenger pigeons *all* morning!"

Clara looked back at her window. At least a dozen pigeons with scrolls were perched on the sill outside.

If Clara didn't know any better, she'd think they also looked a little annoyed.

She scratched her head and let out a huge yawn. "I must've really been out of it. I didn't hear a thing!"

"My father has just given us a

top secret quest!" Lucas said.

Clara pumped her fist. There was nothing she liked more than a royal quest. "Where to?"

"Silvertown," said Lucas.

"The seaport near Mermaid's Cove?" asked Clara. "What happened?"

"A ship disappeared from the

docks last night," Lucas answered. "My father wants us to meet with a captain from the Royal Navy."

"Disappeared? How?"

Prince Lucas shrugged. "That's what we need to find out. We'll meet the captain at a restaurant called the Red Arrow. We have to hurry—good thing you're already dressed and ready to ride!"

Clara looked at herself in the

mirror. She saw that she was still
wearing the same clothes from
yesterday.

Did I forget to change before bed?
she wondered.

Suddenly Clara had the odd feeling she'd forgotten a chunk of yesterday. It was as if she'd skipped from dropping off Zishess to speaking now with Lucas.

"Are you okay?" the prince asked.

"Um, yeah," said Clara. "Sure. Come on. We'd better get going."

The kids were rounding up their horses outside when a strange sound caught Clara's attention.

Screeeeech! Screeeeeech! She looked

up to see the phoenix soaring in the sky. "Is Zishess supposed to be out?"

Lucas adjusted the reins on his horse. "He was getting a bit antsy, so I let him fly free. Besides, we could use an extra pair of eyes on our quest."

Ruskin, who was sitting beside Lucas, snorted.

Clara walked over to him and patted him gently. "Oh, don't you worry, Ruskin. Zishess will never take your place."

Ruskin didn't look very convinced.

"Good dragon," Lucas said as he

hopped on his horse, Ivan. "Now, to Silvertown!"

Clara unhitched her horse, Scallop, from the post near her home.

With their magical creature, Lucas and Clara set off.
The quest was underway!

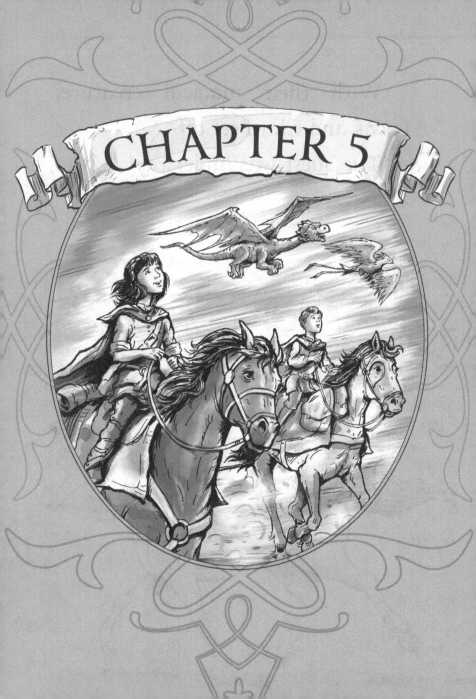

CHAPTER 5

Boatload of Mystery

As Lucas and Clara galloped down the path, Ruskin and Zishess raced through the sky. They screeched and squawked, trying to overtake each other.

"Keep it DOWN!" shouted Lucas. "You'll bring too much attention!"

Clara laughed. "We're traveling

with a scarlet dragon and a magical phoenix. We're bound to be noticed!"

Lucas frowned. "Maybe I

should've left Zishess at home. Truthfully, I don't know what came over me. With one look, it's almost like he *asked* me to bring him."

Soon they entered the Silvertown marketplace. Lucas and Clara tied the horses next to a stone trough filled with water. Zishess and Ruskin landed, sticking to the shadows.

The marketplace bustled with buyers and sellers. There were tables with apples, carrots, potatoes, garlic, and herbs. Sacks of wheat, barley, and oats lay stacked on carts. Lobsters and crab crawled in barrels of seawater.

The kids found the Red Arrow tucked into a hidden corner.

"'No animals allowed,'" said

Clara, reading the sign outside the
restaurant.

Ruskin whimpered.

Lucas shook a finger at the

dragon and the phoenix. "Can we trust you two to stay here until we come back?"

Ruskin and Zishess both huffed. They hadn't warmed to each other, but they both nodded a promise to stay put.

Lucas and Clara walked into the Red Arrow and found an empty table in the corner. Customers laughed and talked noisily.

"How are we supposed to find the captain?" asked Clara. "This place is packed!"

Lucas nodded his head to a man walking toward them. Everything the man wore was large and impressive, from his long coat to his gold belt buckle. Even his dark brown leather boots went up to his knees. On his head he wore a dark hat with a plume of spotted feathers.

"I've never seen a navy captain with a feathered hat before," Clara whispered.

The captain bowed to them before

taking a seat. "Your Highness and Lady Clara—I'm Captain Seabert."

"Nice to meet you!" said Lucas. "We're told your ship has gone missing."

Captain Seabert nodded grimly. "Aye, she was docked at this port and well guarded. But even with security, the ship was stolen under cover of darkness. When my crew came to unload the goods, there was no ship in sight."

Lucas asked, "Does anyone else know about this?"

Captain Seabert looked around

the restaurant suspiciously. "No, and we *must* be careful. My ship holds royal jewels, gold coins, and silver. I don't want them falling into the wrong hands."

"What if they already *are* in the wrong hands?" questioned Clara. "There's been talk of pirates in the area."

Captain Seabert's eyebrows arched. "If it *is* pirates, they're probably far out to sea by now."

Lucas pushed back his chair and stood up. "Then there's no time to waste. We need to look into this right away and ask around for clues."

Clara stood too.

"Thank you for meeting with us,

Captain," she said. "We'll let you know what we find."

Captain Seabert tipped his hat in gratitude.

At the same time, something caught Clara's eye. Dark tendrils of

smoke swirled around another corner of the restaurant. Clara shuddered. *Maybe it's not* who *stole the ship,* she thought. *But rather, what* stole it.

CHAPTER 6

Hide-and-Seek

When Lucas and Clara left the Red Arrow, Ruskin and Zishess were waiting behind a barrel full of flowers.

"We're going to look for clues," said the prince. "Stay close and keep hidden as best you can. I'm not sure who we can trust around here."

Lucas and Clara began to search the docks. Two deckhands rolled a barrel of molasses toward them.

"Excuse me," Lucas asked. "Have you noticed anything suspicious around the docks—maybe even pirates?"

The deckhands bowed before shaking their heads. "No. Just

business as usual, Your Highness."

Lucas and Clara spoke with sailors and crews all along the docks. Nobody knew anything about a missing ship or pirates. But what struck them both as most strange was that no one had heard of Captain Seabert.

"Missing boats are sure hard to track down," said the prince as they finished searching the docks. "They don't leave any evidence."

Clara nodded. "Well, I have a funny feeling there's more to this mystery than we're being told."

"It *is* odd that no one knows Seabert," Lucas agreed. "Maybe he is undercover. Either way, we should keep our guard up. Now, where are our flying friends?"

Lucas whistled for Ruskin and Zishess.

Ruskin bounded from behind a crate and ran to the prince. But the phoenix was nowhere to be found.

Clara was alarmed. "Where *is* Zishess?"

Ruskin shrugged.

Lucas narrowed his eyes at his pet dragon. "Did you scare Zishess away on purpose?"

Ruskin shook his head sharply.

"Tell me the truth," Lucas said in an angrier tone. "We have an important task here! This is no time for a jealous dragon."

Ruskin let out a frustrated whine at that. Then he leaped into the air and flew away in the direction of the castle.

Lucas threw his hands up. "Oh, great! Now we've got two missing creatures *and* a missing ship!"

Clara tried to calm her friend.

"Let's split up," she said. "You go apologize to Ruskin, and I'll search for Zishess. Maybe we'll find clues along the way."

"Okay. Meet back here in an hour?" Lucas asked.

They agreed and took off in separate directions.

As Clara walked through the market, something caught her eye. It wasn't the phoenix, however. It was a set of dark, smoky tendrils lurking in the shadows.

There it is again! she thought.
The coiling smoke seemed to call
to her, and this time Clara followed.

FRESH FISH

CHAPTER 7

Shiver Me Timbers!

"Wait!" Clara cried as she raced after the swirling smoke.

It took off quickly. The dark vapor snaked across the docks and slinked through the marketplace. It twisted through the crowd and beyond the market until finally curling to a stop along the beach below the cliffs.

Clara was quick to keep up, even as her shoes sank into the sand as she ran.

"Got you!" Clara said as she reached the smoke tendrils.

They had led her into a grotto. She peered inside and gasped. There was a ship with tattered flags and the royal seal.

"This must be Seabert's ship! But what's it doing here?" Clara whispered.

She watched the shadow tendrils swoosh up a wooden gangplank and onto the deck.

Clara snuck over to the gangplank. Then she stopped to listen. The ship was quiet, except for water gently lapping against the hull.

Nobody's here, Clara thought. Carefully she crept up the wooden plank and boarded the ship. As soon as her feet landed on the deck, somebody stepped out from behind a tall crate.

"Halt!" boomed a voice. "Who goes there?"

Clara's heart pounded against her ribs. It was Captain Seabert!

"It's just me!" she cried.

Captain Seabert pulled off his feathered hat and bowed.

"My apologies, Lady Clara!" he said. "It seems, after we parted, a bird as bright as the sun led me to my missing ship!"

Clara's mind spun wildly. *He's talking about Zishess! The phoenix must have flown off on his own and found the ship first. But . . . why wouldn't he come back to find us?*

"Have you found the royal cargo?" Clara asked.

Captain Seabert smiled broadly. "The cargo is safe below deck," he replied, his hand showing the way.

A feeling of unease grew in Clara's stomach. *Should I trust Captain Seabert?*

"I'll wait for Prince Lucas," she

said. "He'll be here any moment . . . with the king's knights."

The captain's smile disappeared. He snapped his fingers. Trapdoors creaked open. Boots scuffed across the floorboards. From all corners, they were surrounded by pirates.

"Look out, Captain!" cried Clara. "It's a trap!"

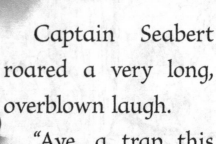

Captain Seabert roared a very long, overblown laugh.

"Aye, a trap this be!" he cried gleefully. "And you, my dear, have been CAUGHT. Though 'tis a prince I'd wanted!"

Clara stepped back, beginning to put everything together. "No wonder not a single person has heard of a Captain Seabert. You're nothing but a greedy pirate with a stolen royal ship! Mark my word, you'll *never* catch Lucas!"

Captain Seabert let out a wicked chuckle. "Don't be so sure. See, I have something he can't live without: the Lady Clara, his greatest friend."

Wings flapped, and the phoenix landed on the pirate's shoulder. Seabert stroked the phoenix's feathers.

"Zishess?" Clara whispered in surprise. "No . . . he's on *our* side."

"Who do you think sent the phoenix to the castle?" asked the pirate captain. "This creature is under a spell and answers only to me. And thanks to you, he's heard all the king's secrets while he sat in the throne room."

The rest of the pirate crew laughed loudly.

Clara clenched her fists. It all made sense now. She had been hypnotized to place Zishess in the throne room. Even Lucas had been under a spell to bring the phoenix to Silvertown.

"You won't get away with this, Seabert," said Clara.

A horrible grin spread on Seabert's face. "I don't expect to get away with just you, my dear. Your prince will be here soon. Until then—"

The captain waved to his pirate crew and said, "Lock her up!"

Together Again

"*Ru-u-u-u-skin!*" called the prince as he wandered over grassy hills. "Ruskin, where are you?!"

The upset dragon was nowhere to be found.

Lucas knew his trusted friend would come back eventually, but he felt bad about hurting his feelings. He didn't know where Zishess was, but that didn't mean Ruskin had anything to do with it.

I blew it! the prince thought. *Father will be so disappointed.*

Then Lucas felt a rush of wind behind him. He whirled around to see his scarlet friend.

The prince threw his arms around Ruskin. "I'm so sorry about what I said. I didn't mean it, I promise!"

But Ruskin wiggled out of Lucas's hug and nudged the prince forward sharply.

"Whoa, Ruskin! What's wrong?" Lucas asked.

The dragon roared loudly and pranced about impatiently. Lucas had no idea what was bothering his dragon so much.

"Did you find Zishess?" he asked.

Ruskin shook his head.

"I wish you could talk," Lucas joked. "Are you hungry?"

Ruskin paused to consider this.

Then he shook his head quickly.

Then Lucas asked, "Is Clara in trouble?"

This time Ruskin roared in agreement.

"Oh no!" Lucas cried. "Lead the way, Ruskin, quick!"

Ruskin soared into the air and flew toward the Silvertown cliffs. He landed on the beach by the grotto. When Lucas caught up to him, the dragon nodded his head toward the cave. Together they peered inside.

"Great job, Ruskin!" said Lucas. "You've found the missing ship. And,

look, there's a whole crew on it. But they don't look like the Royal Navy. They look like . . . pirates!"

He watched as a captive was taken below deck.

"That's Clara!" he cried out. "She's been captured!"

The prince quickly formed a plan. "Ruskin, can you carry me to the lower deck? I'll sneak in through a port opening."

Ruskin did as Lucas asked.

"Stay close in case I need your help," the prince whispered. Then he squeezed through one of the port openings and landed on the floorboards with a thunk.

"Well, well, well—Prince Lucas!"

a sneering voice said. "How lovely for you to join us."

Prince Lucas slowly stood up. "Seabert—you've been playing us the whole time!"

The captain laughed so hard that
Zishess almost slid off his shoulder.
"That I have. And you will draw
me a fine ransom. The king's gold
will soon be mine."

CHAPTER 9

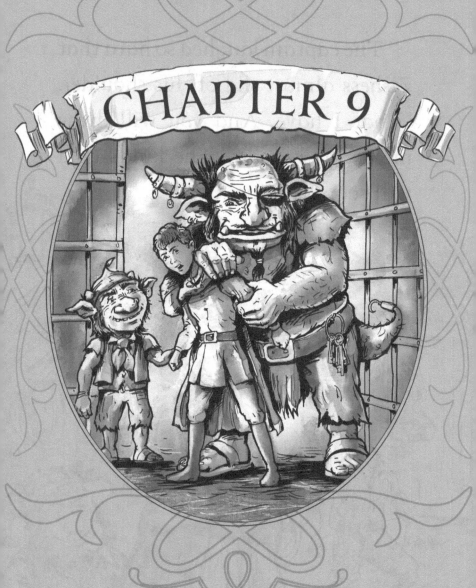

Seas the Day!

The pirates tossed Lucas into the ship's jail with Clara.

"I told you he'd show up," said Seabert with a laugh. "Now let's get this show on the road . . . or rather, out to sea!"

The pirates left the kids alone.

"Lucas!" Clara cried out. "You shouldn't have come."

"You're my best friend!" Lucas said. "You'd do it for me too."

Suddenly the ship tilted side to side. They were beginning to move.

"We're sailing!" Clara said. "We're trapped on a pirate ship, and no one knows we're here."

A dark feeling of dread fell over them. Then a real darkness began to bloom.

"Look!" whispered Lucas as swirling shadows moved toward them. The tendrils assembled themselves into a humanlike form that stood outside the cell.

"It's a Nameless Messenger," whispered Clara. "*You're* the one I've been following! What are you doing here?"

The Nameless Messenger stretched out his smoky arms and handed Clara a bow and a quiver of arrows—*her* arrows! He also gave her a vial filled with a shimmering potion.

Lucas bowed his head. "Thank you, Nameless Messenger."

In a chilling, ghostly voice the Nameless Messenger said, "You have friends in high places."

Then he vanished.

Lucas inspected the shimmering vial. "This looks like a potion from the wizards. I wonder what it's for."

Clara pocketed it. "I have a feeling our phoenix friend will need it. But first, we need to get out of here."

As the ship continued its sway, Clara nocked an arrow with a rope attached to it. Then she raised her bow and took aim at a set of keys hanging on the opposite wall outside the cell.

"If only this boat would stay still," Lucas groaned.

"Don't worry," Clara said. "A good friend built a fantastic archery course."

She sent the arrow flying, and it struck in the middle of the key ring.

"You really are Wrenly's greatest archer," Lucas cheered.

Clara pulled the keys toward them on the rope and unlocked the door. Lucas and Clara raced to a porthole, out of which they could see Ruskin flying back and forth.

"Meet us up top!" Lucas whispered.

The ever-ready dragon nodded.

Lucas and Clara crept up to the
ship's deck.

"Hey, *Captain*!" Clara shouted.

Captain Seabert and the pirates
jumped in alarm when they saw the
kids had escaped from the ship's jail.

"Can pirates *swim*?" asked Clara.
The stunned pirates looked at one

another. "Pirates can dog-paddle!" one of them said.

"Sometimes we hang on to a dolphin's fin," another added.

Seabert roared, "Enough! Seize them!"

But Lucas was ready. He let out a loud whistle and shouted, "Ruskin, NOW!"

CHAPTER 10

Into the Briny Deep

Ruskin zoomed over the deck and whisked the pirates overboard.

Splish! Splash! Splosh!

The ocean swallowed them up, and one by one, they bobbed to the surface.

"Dog-paddle, mates!" cried a soggy pirate. Another spluttered as he swam to shore.

Seabert, who was still on board, clutched the wheel of the ship.

"Enchant them, Zishess!" the captain ordered the phoenix.

The bird obeyed the command and swooped toward Lucas and Clara. Zishess's eyes glowed like hot embers.

Clara threw the potion vial to Lucas. He popped off the cork and held it up.

Zishess screeched, snatched the vial in his beak, and drank it fully.

112

Sparkles shimmered around the bird's body and then flew outward like fireworks. Zishess screeched again, only this time it was a screech of freedom.

"The captain's spell has been broken!" Clara cried.

Then the phoenix turned on Seabert. The pirate held up his hands to protect himself.

"Nice fire birdie!" he said, gulping. "You wouldn't hurt your master! Remember how I raised you from a teeny-tiny flame and fed you all those worms?"

The phoenix hovered in front of the captain. His blazing feathered body began to grow. It grew until the phoenix became a magnificent fire bird, raging with a fearsome beauty. The phoenix clutched Seabert's collar in his talons and flew away.

115

Lucas and Clara watched in wonder as the phoenix headed toward the horizon . . . where a royal ship approached.

"That's one of my father's ships!" cried Lucas. "Help is here!"

They watched as Zishess reached the ship and dropped Seabert onto the deck.

When Zishess returned, Ruskin approached. Instead of growling, Ruskin bowed his head.

"Thank you, Zishess," said Clara. "You've charred the evil captain's hopes and dreams—just like in the scroll!"

The phoenix bowed his scarlet head, screeched a good-bye, and soared back into the air. The kids watched until the extraordinary bird's fiery wings blended into the sun.

"Do you think he'll ever come back?" Clara asked.

Lucas smiled. "I hope so. Either way, he'll always be welcome in the kingdom of Wrenly."